SHINO
AND THE CHAOS
CREW

The
DAY TECH
TOOK OVER

Written by Chris Callaghan

Illustrated by Amit Tayal

Collins

Shinoy and the Chaos Crew

When Shinoy downloads the Chaos Crew app on his phone, a glitch in the system gives him the power to summon his TV heroes into his world.

With the team on board, Shinoy can figure out what dastardly plans the red-eyed S.N.A.I.R., a Super Nasty Artificial Intelligent Robot, has come up with, and save the day.

"That was impossible!" sighed Toby, showing Shinoy his unfinished homework.

Shinoy grinned and waved his completed worksheets.

Toby's mouth fell open. "But how? I didn't even understand the questions."

"It was easy," bragged Shinoy. He knew he shouldn't boast but it felt good. He'd struggled with this topic, but suddenly it all made sense.

1. $5x = 40$

   $x = 8$

2. $\dfrac{x}{9} = 7$

   $x = 63$

3. $\dfrac{x}{7} = 8$

   $x = 56$

4. $x + 19 = 26$

   $x = 7$

The class was getting restless.

"Where's Miss Sharp?" Toby asked. "It must be after nine."

Shinoy looked at his watch.

"Cool watch – is that new?"

"It's a smart watch. I got it online with my birthday money from a pop-up recommendation. It tells me how many steps I make, every breath I take, my heart rate and even my brain activity."

Its display danced with whirling white dots.

"It wouldn't show much activity in my brain," yawned Toby. "It's far too early."

Mr Amitri, the head teacher, bounded into the room and scribbled on the whiteboard.

"I'm taking this lesson today and I'm going to show you the beauty of Maths."

"This is a very important equation. I don't expect you to understand it," Mr Amitri said, "but try to see its simple beauty."

Shinoy immediately knew the equation was wrong. "I'm sorry, sir, but I don't think that's right."

Mr Amitri made one of his "I am not amused" looks, but Shinoy continued: "It should be *plus* one, not *multiply* by one."

Mr Amitri glanced at his notes. "Er, that's right. How did you know that?"

Shinoy shrugged.

Toby whispered, "Smarty pants with your smarty watch!"

The dancing dots on Shinoy's watch had turned red.

7

For the rest of the lesson, Shinoy was unstoppable.

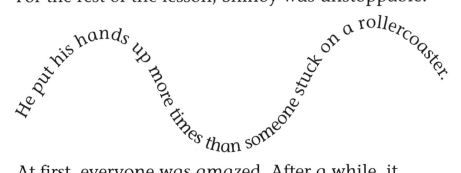

He put his hands up more times than someone stuck on a rollercoaster.

At first, everyone was amazed. After a while, it became a bit boring. Then it was just plain annoying.

"Why don't we let someone else have a go?"
Mr Amitri kept saying.

Even Toby added, "Come on, Shinoy, have
a breather!"

Everyone was relieved when it was breaktime.

In the playground, Shinoy pointed out the names of all the trees, how long they lived for and what animals could be found in them.

$$D = \frac{\pi R^3 \rho \omega}{vm} x^2$$

When Toby suggested that they kick a ball about, Shinoy explained the angles and force you needed to get the ball into the goal. What had happened to his friend, wondered Toby?

"Maybe we should call the Chaos Crew?" suggested Toby. "You always do that when something weird happens."

"It's not weird that I'm cleverer than you," Shinoy snapped. He stomped off leaving Toby feeling hurt and confused. Something was definitely wrong.

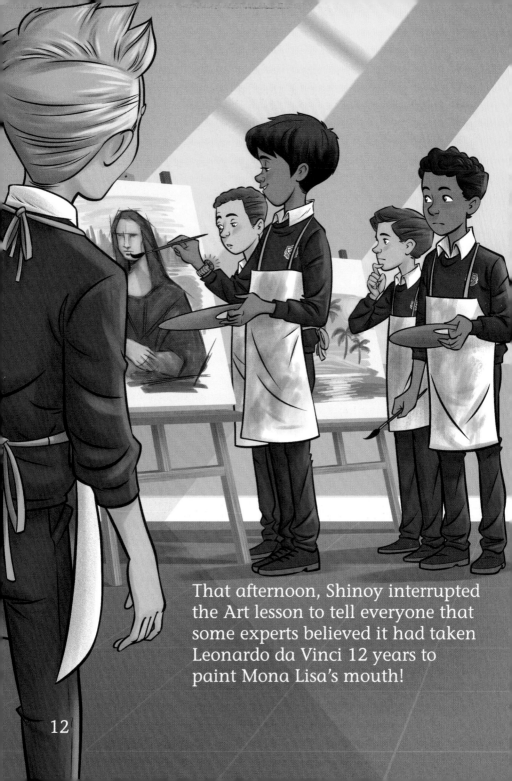

That afternoon, Shinoy interrupted the Art lesson to tell everyone that some experts believed it had taken Leonardo da Vinci 12 years to paint Mona Lisa's mouth!

Toby noticed Shinoy's rucksack dangling over his chair. After a quick rummage, he carefully removed Shinoy's mobile phone. He didn't feel good about it but he needed to do something.

Outside the school gates, Shinoy scratched equations on to the pavement with chalk.

"Why don't we go to mine and play Chaos Crew on the GameStation?" pleaded Toby.

Shinoy's watch glowed red. "And take that watch off. It's doing things to your brain."

Shinoy growled, "You're just jealous of my watch and my brain. Leave me alone!"

This was serious. Toby pressed the app on Shinoy's phone. "Call to Action, Chaos Crew!" He'd always wanted to do that but he wished it had been for a different reason.

Bug, the Chaos Crew's tech wizard, stepped out from a flash of light. "What's up, Toby? Is Shinoy OK?"

"No, he's not. His brain's got so big it's making him act like a spoiled muppet."

"How did you get here?" demanded Shinoy. "I didn't summon you!"

"See what I mean! His watch is messing with his head."

Bug flipped down a scanning screen from her headset. "That's Further Earth tech," she said, "with S.N.A.I.R.'s nasty colouring."

"You took my phone!" Shinoy yelled, making a lunge for it. He and Toby scuffled together.

"Ha! I got it," Shinoy sneered, holding up his phone.

"And I got this," grinned Toby, holding the smart watch.

Toby grabbed a rock. "I'll smash it!"

"No!" screamed Shinoy. "It's mine!"

"But it's changed you. I want my friend back."

"It's making me clever," Shinoy pleaded. "I'll be able to do all my schoolwork, just like my sister, Myra! I'll pass all my exams."

"But I won't have my friend."

Shinoy had no answer to that and his anger faded.

Toby held the rock high above the watch and froze.
He couldn't do it. "It's not mine to break."
He handed the watch back.

Shinoy dropped the watch on to the ground. He took the rock from Toby and tried to smash the watch, but it didn't make a scratch. The red lights blinked brighter than before. "I can't break it!"

Bug grinned and pointed a finger of her Chaos Crew Quantum Gauntlet at it.

"I told you – it's tech from Further Earth. It'll take more than a rock." The lights fizzled and faded from the watch.

"You could have done that before, when I was still wearing it."

Bug nodded. "Yes, but I knew you could deal with it. Sometimes friendship is stronger than any tech in the universe."

"I'm sorry," Shinoy said. "I was horrible today."

Toby smiled. "Before your brain goes completely back to normal, could you help me with my homework?"

Time out

Ideas for reading

Written by Clare Dowdall, PhD
Lecturer and Primary Literacy Consultant

Reading objectives

- discuss the sequence of events in books and how items of information are related
- make inferences on the basis of what is being said and done
- answer and ask questions
- predict what might happen on the basis of what has been read so far

Spoken language objectives

- maintain attention and participate actively in collaborative conversations, staying on topic and initiating and responding to comments
- participate in discussions, presentations, performances and debates

Curriculum links: Mathematics – number problems; PSHE – relationships: friendship

Word count: 961

Interest words: equation, angles, Leonardo da Vinci, Mona Lisa, Quantum Gauntlet.

Resources: pencils and paper, ICT for recording a video diary

Build a context for reading

- Read the book's title *The Day Tech Took Over*. Ask children to explain what 'tech' is short for, and discuss the types of technology they can think of.
- Look at the front cover and read the blurb together. Ask children to suggest what might be happening to Shinoy.
- Read through the interest words, and help with decoding and pronunciation, in preparation for story reading: *equation, angles, Leonardo da Vinci, Mona Lisa, Quantum Gauntlet*

Understand and apply reading strategies

- Ask children to read pp2–7 silently, noticing what is happening, and how Shinoy and Toby are getting on as friends.

Kangaroos

Written by Martin Waddell
Illustrated by Frank James

Kate saw a small kangaroo
on a trip to the zoo.
'I want one too!' said Kate.

So she went to the shops and
she bought herself one.

It slept in the kitchen
so that was all right.

But . . .

it grew,

and it grew,

and it **grew**,
the way kangaroos do.

It kept bouncing about and knocking
the pans on the floor and it grew too big
to bounce through the door so . . .

Kate knocked a hole
in the wall to the garden.

The kangaroo bounced and it bounced and it bounced and it bounced and it bounced and it bounced – the way kangaroos do. The boy next-door saw Kate's kangaroo. 'I want one too,' he said.

So Kate went to the shops for a new
kangaroo to give to the boy next-door.

That made two –
kangaroo – kangaroo –
one at each side of the fence.

The kangaroos knocked the fence down,
which made a big garden to bounce in.
So that was all right, but, one night . . .

... along came the kangaroos' cousins!

They were bouncing and

bouncing and

bouncing and

bouncing

and

bouncing about.

Then out of the pouches
came small kangaroos
who did little hops and
fell over and cried for
their mummies.

17

The people who lived in the street
were scared of the kangaroo feet.
So they locked their doors and
hid in their houses.

Next day when the people looked out,
the kangaroos were all gone!
So was Kate.
So that seemed all right but . . .

next day, Kate came back to the street
with a small crocodile.

Kate's crocodile had such a nice smile
that everyone liked it.
So that was all right but . . .

it grew and

it grew, and it grew

the way crocodiles do and . . .

it had cousins too!